MR. CLUMSY

by Roger Hargreaves

It was a rather nice morning.

In the sky the sun was up.

Shining.

In the trees the birds were up.

Singing.

But, in a rather scruffy house in the middle of a field, somebody wasn't up.

Can you guess who that somebody might be?

His alarm clock went off.

Mr Clumsy woke up, and reached out an arm to switch off his alarm clock.

And knocked it on to the floor.

"Whoops," he said. "That's the third alarm clock I've broken this week."

Mr Clumsy, as you might have guessed, was a rather clumsy fellow.

He got out of bed and switched on the radio.

The knob came off in his hand.

"Whoops," he said. "That's the second radio I've broken this month."

He went downstairs.

The postman had been, and there was a letter waiting for Mr Clumsy, lying on his doormat.

He picked it up, and went into his kitchen.

"First things first," he said, and took a slice of bread out of his bread bin and popped it into his toaster.

"Now," he thought,"I wonder who this letter is from?"

He looked at the letter in his hand.

But the letter wasn't in his hand.

What was in his hand was a slice of bread!

"I don't understand it," he said. "Where's the letter gone?"

Can you guess where the letter had gone?

That's right!

He'd put the letter in the toaster instead of the bread!

And there it was, browning nicely.

"Whoops," he said fishing it out.

"Ouch," he said, dropping it. "It's hot!"

Mr Clumsy bent down to pick the letter up.

But, in doing so, he banged his forehead on his kitchen table, and in doing so, he fell forwards and got his head stuck in the bread bin!

All of which wasn't surprising really.

As we said, he was a rather clumsy fellow.

In fact, he was a very clumsy fellow.

Actually, he was the clumsiest person in the world!

That very same morning, after he'd managed to get the bread bin off his head, Mr Clumsy went to town.

Shopping.

"First things first," he said, and went into the bank to get some money.

And somehow, while he was in the bank, Mr Clumsy, while he was writing a cheque, managed to spill ink all over the bank manager.

"Whoops," said Mr Clumsy.

He went into the butcher's.

"Morning Butcher," he said, cheerily.

And then he somehow managed to trip over his shoelaces, and somehow managed to fall into the butcher's shop window, and somehow managed to finish up with a string of sausages round his neck!

"Whoops," he said.

Mr Clumsy's next call was the supermarket.

Just inside the door there was a huge pyramid pile of cans of soup.

Well.

You can imagine what happened, can't you?

"Mmm," exclaimed Mr Clumsy. "Soup would be nice for supper," and he picked up a can.

Not a can from the top of the pile.

Oh no, not Mr Clumsy.

"Whoops," said Mr Clumsy, and went on his way.

Rubbing his head.

On his way home, he called in at the farm for some eggs.

And somehow, while he was crossing the farmyard, he managed to trip up.

And somehow, as he was falling, he managed to grab hold of the farmer.

And somehow, they both managed to finish up in the duck pond!

SPLASH!

"Whoops," said Mr Clumsy.

"Please," said the farmer as they sat together in the duck pond. "In future can I deliver your eggs to you?"

"That's extraordinarily kind of you," replied Mr Clumsy.

"Don't mention it," muttered the farmer.

Mr Clumsy went home.

"First things first," he said, and went for a bath.

But, as he was stepping into his bath, his foot somehow managed to slip on the soap, and he somehow managed to turn a somersault, and he somehow managed to land with his head in the linen basket.

"Whoops!" said a muffled voice.

Later, he went downstairs for supper.

Soup, from the supermarket.

Sausages, from the butcher's.

And eggs, from the farm.

Or rather.

Soup, from the saucepan that had boiled over.

Sausages, from the frying pan that had caught fire.

And eggs, oh dear, very very very scrambled eggs!

A normal Mr Clumsy sort of supper.

"That was nice," he said, leaning back in his chair.

CRASH!

"Whoops!" said Mr Clumsy, "I think I'd better go to bed."

And he did.

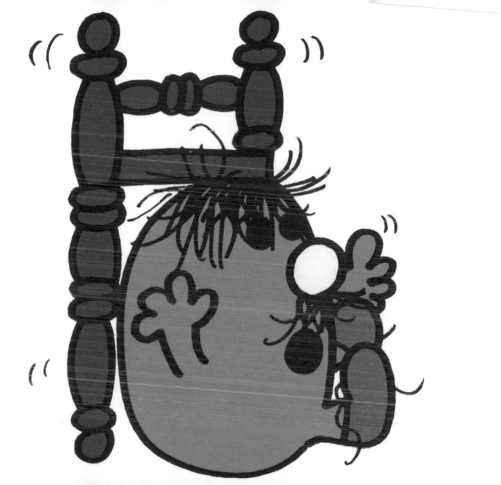

And that is the end of the story.

"Goodnight, Mr Clumsy!"

Mr Clumsy leaned over to turn off his bedside light, and . . .

Oh dear.

"Whoops!"

3 Great Offers for MR. MEN Fans!

MR. MEN TOKEN

1 New Mr. Men or Little Miss Library Bus Presentation Cases

A brand new stronger, roomier school bus library box, with sturdy carrying handle and stay-closed fasteners.

The full colour, wipe-clean boxes make a great home for your full collection.

They're just £5.99 inc P&P and free bookmark!

☐ MR. MEN ☐ LITTLE MISS (please tick and order overleaf)

2 Door Hangers and Posters

In every Mr. Men and Little Miss book like this one, you will find a special token. Collect 6 tokens and we will send you a brilliant Mr. Men or Little Miss poster and a Mr. Men or Little Miss double sided full colour bedroom door hanger of your choice. Simply tick your choice in the list and tape a 50p coin for your two items to this page.

PLEASE STICK YOUR 50P COIN HERE

Door Hangers (please tick)
☐ Mr. Nosey & Mr. Muddle
☐ Mr. Slow & Mr. Busy
☐ Mr. Messy & Mr. Quiet
☐ Mr. Perfect & Mr. Forgetful
☐ Little Miss Fun & Little Miss Late
☐ Little Miss Helpful & Little Miss Tidy
☐ Little Miss Busy & Little Miss Brainy
☐ Little Miss Star & Little Miss Fun

Posters (please tick)
☐ MR.MEN
☐ LITTLE MISS

3 Sixteen Beautiful Fridge Magnets – any 2 for £2.00! inc.P&P

They're very special collector's items!
Simply tick your first and second* choices from the list below
of any 2 characters!

1st Choice
- ☐ Mr. Happy
- ☐ Mr. Lazy
- ☐ Mr. Topsy-Turvy
- ☐ Mr. Bounce
- ☐ Mr. Bump
- ☐ Mr. Small
- ☐ Mr. Snow
- ☐ Mr. Wrong
- ☐ Mr. Daydream
- ☐ Mr. Tickle
- ☐ Mr. Greedy
- ☐ Mr. Funny
- ☐ Little Miss Giggles
- ☐ Little Miss Splendid
- ☐ Little Miss Naughty
- ☐ Little Miss Sunshine

2nd Choice
- ☐ Mr. Happy
- ☐ Mr. Lazy
- ☐ Mr. Topsy-Turvy
- ☐ Mr. Bounce
- ☐ Mr. Bump
- ☐ Mr. Small
- ☐ Mr. Snow
- ☐ Mr. Wrong
- ☐ Mr. Daydream
- ☐ Mr. Tickle
- ☐ Mr. Greedy
- ☐ Mr. Funny
- ☐ Little Miss Giggles
- ☐ Little Miss Splendid
- ☐ Little Miss Naughty
- ☐ Little Miss Sunshine

*Only in case your first choice is out of stock.

--- **TO BE COMPLETED BY AN ADULT** ---

**To apply for any of these great offers, ask an adult to complete the coupon below and send it with
the appropriate payment and tokens, if needed, to MR. MEN OFFERS, PO BOX 7, MANCHESTER M19 2HD**

☐ Please send ____ Mr. Men Library case(s) and/or ____ Little Miss Library case(s) at £5.99 each inc P&P
☐ Please send a poster and door hanger as selected overleaf. I enclose six tokens plus a 50p coin for P&P
☐ Please send me ____ pair(s) of Mr. Men/Little Miss fridge magnets, as selected above at £2.00 inc P&P

Fan's Name _____

Address _____

_____ **Postcode** _____

Date of Birth _____

Name of Parent/Guardian _____

Total amount enclosed £ _____

☐ **I enclose a cheque/postal order payable to Egmont Books Limited**

☐ **Please charge my MasterCard/Visa/Amex/Switch or Delta account** (delete as appropriate)

Card Number

Expiry date ____ / ____   **Signature** _____

MR.MEN   LITTLE MISS
Mr. Men and Little Miss™ & ©Mrs. Roger Hargreaves

CUT ALONG DOTTED LINE AND RETURN THIS WHOLE PAGE